Aa Bb Cc Dd Ee Ff Gg

1234567890

Hh Ii Jj Kk Ll

Mm Nn Oo Pp Qq Rr

Rocky and the Lamb

and the

For my daughter Pepa
G. G.

For Ava
L. C.

First edition for the United States and Canada published in
2006 by Barron's Educational Series, Inc.

Text © Greg Gormley 2006
Illustrations © Lynne Chapman 2006

The right of Greg Gormley and Lynne Chapman to be identified as
the author and illustrator of this work
has been asserted by them in accordance with the
Copyright, Designs and Patents Act, 1988.

First published in Great Britain in 2006 by
Gullane Children's Books, an imprint of
Pinwheel Limited
Winchester House – 4th floor
259-269 Old Marylebone Road
London NW1 5XJ

All inquiries should be addressed to:
Barron's Educational Series, Inc.
250 Wireless Boulevard
Hauppauge, NY 11788
http://www.barronseduc.com

Library of Congress Control Number 2005929091

ISBN-13: 978-0-7641-5939-8
ISBN-10: 0-7641-5939-9

Printed in China
9 8 7 6 5 4 3 2 1

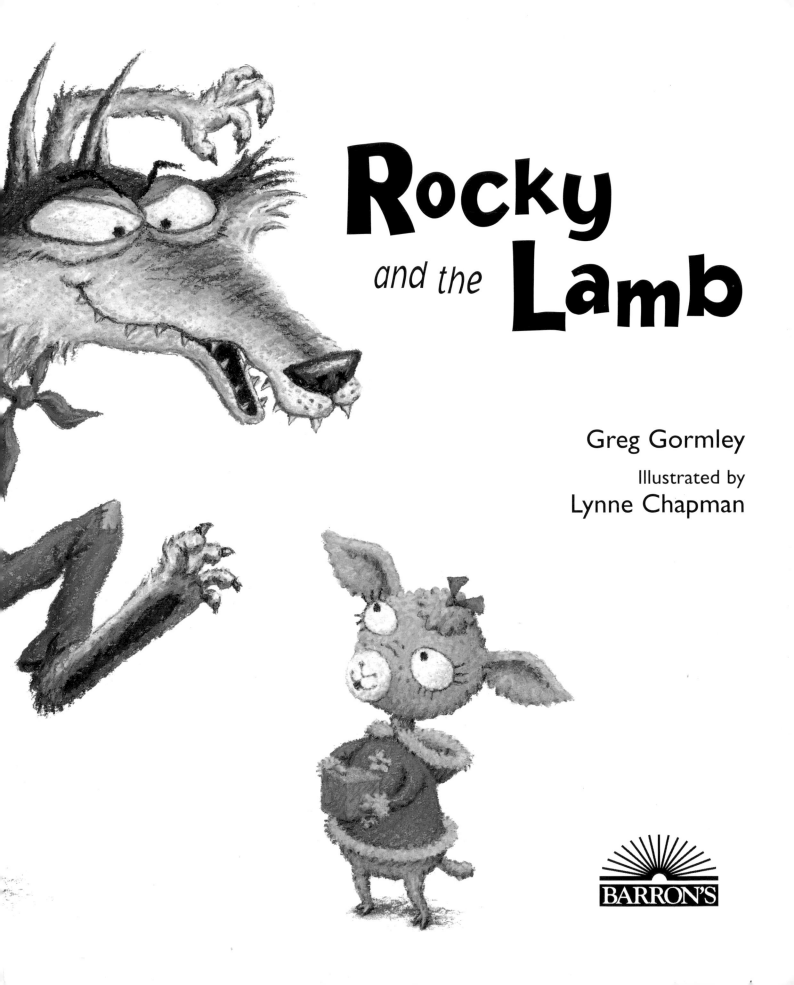

Rocky
and the Lamb

Greg Gormley

Illustrated by
Lynne Chapman

BARRON'S

In a misty, murky, far-off land, a gloomy mountain stood.
At the mountain's thorny foot, in a lonely stony pass,
behind a boulder, lived a wolf called Rocky. He was not
a noble or a handsome beast. Mean and cowardly as
a dog at bath time, Rocky was a horrible bully.

As travelers trudged through the pass, Rocky
would steal their valuables, or even their
non-valuables. Indeed, Rocky would
steal anything at all.

If he met a small animal carrying something nice, he would say, "Hey Shorty, hand it over," in the most menacing way possible. But if a large creature traveled by, no matter how tempting their belongings looked, the wolf would hide behind his rock and let them pass.

One day Rocky spied a sweet little lamb making her
way along the path. She was carrying a small, plain box.
"How nice," said Rocky to himself.
"A present for me."

As the lamb drew closer, the wolf sprang out.
"Hey, marshmallow-face," he snarled. "What's in the box?"
"A splendid crown for the king's birthday," said the lamb, who
was polite and shy but not at all afraid. "It is guarded by the
scariest, hairiest monster you could possibly imagine."
"Oh, well, the palace is, er . . . that way,"
lied Rocky pointing to a little mountain path.

I'll find a way to get that splendid crown, he thought.

The path wound upward and up and up again,
toward the very peak of the mountain. Delicately, the
lamb tiptoed in and out of the scratching, scraping
thorn bushes that covered the mountainside.
"**Ee, ow, ouch!**" cried Rocky as he tried to follow.

Next the lamb skipped in and out of the crashing, bashing rocks.

Bink,

bonk,

donk!

bounced the rocks and stones off poor Rocky's head.

PALACE THIS WAY

Finally, the lamb stepped lightly over deep mounds of snow.
"**Brrr,**" shivered Rocky as he landed in the middle
of a snowbank, right up to his neck.

Meanwhile, the lamb had reached the top of the
mountain and the end of the path. Finding no
palace, she shrugged her shoulders and sat down.

Carefully she opened the magic box and . . .

. . . took out her lunch of fresh bread, a juicy
green apple, and a jug of creamy milk to drink.

There was indeed a most splendid crown,
which she placed on a small satin cushion,
but no sign at all of a monster.

Aha! There never was a monster, thought Rocky,
I'm taking that crown. But by the time he had
struggled free of the snow, the lamb had
already set off on her way again.

The lamb walked softly over the freezing snow. Rocky
waded after her sputtering and shuddering –
he was so **c-c-cold** and **wet**.

With a hop, skip, and a dainty pirouette, the lamb passed each falling rock untouched. But every lump seemed to clobber Rocky no matter how he dodged and weaved.

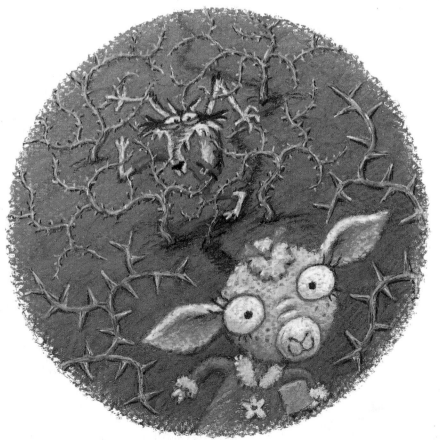

Between those terrible thorns the lamb slipped completely unscathed, but every single spike seemed to catch and tear at Rocky until he was so tender that he yelped. But the lamb didn't hear a thing, and she just skipped merrily along.

At last Rocky caught up with the lamb.
"Oh, Mr. Wolf, I got lost! How kind of you to
come and help me," said the lamb, happy to see him.
"I'll help you in a minute. Now give me that box,"
growled the wolf.

Rocky snatched the
box and lifted the lid.
"Mr. Wolf, wait—" began the
lamb, but it was too late . . .

Out of the box flew the
scariest,
hairiest
monster
you could possibly imagine!

The monster chased Rocky through the scratching, scraping thorns, "**Ow!**"

The monster chased Rocky through the crashing, bashing rocks, **Donk!**

The monster chased Rocky through the
f-f-freezing deep snow, "**Brrr!**"

The monster chased Rocky up and down
and around the mountains for miles and miles.

Finally, cornered behind his very own boulder, Rocky
whimpered, "Please don't hurt me, scary monster,
I promise I'll be a good wolf."

At that moment the
lamb appeared . . .

"I'm so sorry," she said to Rocky. "Leave Mr. Wolf alone, you naughty monster! He was only trying to help me get to the palace." The monster slunk back into the box looking a little ashamed.

Having apologized again and thanking Rocky for his kindness, the lamb continued on to the palace where she told everyone about the nice Mr. Wolf.

As for Rocky, he was so sorry for his wickedness, not to mention his bruises, that he kept his promise and became a good wolf.

So many of the creatures who had talked to the lamb asked for his help when passing through the mountains that Rocky became a famous mountain guide and never robbed anyone ever again.

The End